After Peaches

MICHELLE MULDER

ORCA BOOK PUBLISHERS

Library and Archives Canada Cataloguing in Publication

Mulder, Michelle
After peaches / written by Michelle Mulder.
(Orca young readers)

Issued in print and electronic formats.
ISBN 978-1-55469-176-0 (pbk.).—ISBN 978-1-55469-177-7 (pdf).—
ISBN 978-1-55469-432-7 (epub)

I. Title.
PS8626.U435A64 2009   jC813'.6   C2009-902807-7

First published in the United States, 2009
Library of Congress Control Number: 2009928213

Summary: Rosario and her parents come to Canada as political refugees from Mexico. Rosario hates her heavily accented English, but she breaks the language barrier to save a migrant farm worker's life.

MIX
Paper from
responsible sources
FSC® C016245

Orca Book Publishers is dedicated to preserving the environment and has printed this book on Forest Stewardship Council® certified paper.

Orca Book Publishers gratefully acknowledges the support for its publishing programs provided by the following agencies: the Government of Canada through the Canada Book Fund and the Canada Council for the Arts, and the Province of British Columbia through the BC Arts Council and the Book Publishing Tax Credit.

Cover artwork by Simon Ng
Author photo by David Lowes

ORCA BOOK PUBLISHERS
www.orcabook.com

Printed and bound in Canada.

20 19 18 17 • 8 7 6 5

For those with the courage to speak

Contents

CHAPTER 1

The Plan

"Hey, stupid!" The voice came from behind me.

I didn't need to turn around to know it was Robbie Zec, standing at the edge of the schoolyard with his buddies. They always yelled at me at the end of the day, when teachers couldn't hear and probably didn't care.

I didn't yell back anymore, just pulled myself taller and smiled at Julie as we crossed the street toward her place.

"Julie's mum's hired you to clean their house, eh?" Robbie called. "It's about time you got a job. You can't mooch off the government forever."

I flinched, and Julie linked her arm with mine before I could bolt back to the school and knock him over.

The astonished look on his face would have been worth getting in trouble for, I thought. He would never expect a girl to attack him. And I think Julie would have been secretly proud of me. She had been Robbie's victim before I arrived, because she was way smarter than anyone else in grade four. Now he picked on me because he thought I was way dumber.

"Ignore them," Julie whispered, locking her elbow tighter with mine.

"I'm trying," I hissed back.

Julie was the only kid I ever spoke English to. With all the other kids, I was silent, and everyone thought it was because I still spoke English like a two-year-old. That's what Robbie said when I first came to school in January, and I yelled at him in Spanish then. I used every bad word I knew, and when I ran out, I shouted the Spanish names of vegetables because he wouldn't know the difference anyway. I liked the scared look on his face, and the next day half of Georgison Elementary was whispering that I'd put a Mexican curse on Robbie's family. They never found out the truth, and only Julie knew what I'd really said. After that day in February, I decided not to talk at school anymore.

On my first day of silence, our teacher, Ms. Bower, made me stay after class to tell her why I'd stopped talking. I broke my vow just that once and told her the truth—that I didn't want the other kids to make fun of my English. She said I shouldn't let it bother me and that practicing was the only way to improve, but she wasn't going to push me. I knew she was one of those teachers who wanted everyone to like her, and I think she was a little afraid of Robbie and his buddies too.

The next day she told the class what a brave person I was to come to Canada and learn a new language, and that everyone should help me with my English. Robbie and his friends laughed at that idea, but she ignored them and went on with our math lesson. From then on, she only ever asked me questions I could answer with "yes" or "no."

Now it was early May, and only Julie knew that my English was getting better each day. By September, I was going to speak completely fluent Canadian English. Everyone would be amazed, and Robbie would be the one who was speechless.

"She's so dumb, she probably can't understand what we're saying," Robbie shouted, practically in my ear. They were following close enough to step on our heels.

Julie and I kept walking arm in arm, and she talked as though nothing unusual was happening. That was the very best thing about Julie: no matter how crazy she thought I was for not speaking English at school, she always stuck by me...even when people were yelling insults in our ears.

"Wait till I tell you about my plan for this summer," Julie said. I looked at her, surprised. Neither of us liked talking about the summer. Julie was going to be with her father in a big-city skyscraper for two months, and I'd be here, working at the farm with my parents. Neither of us would have any friends close by, and once Julie left for Vancouver, I probably wouldn't speak to her until September. Even if we could have afforded the long-distance calls, I hated speaking English on the phone. It was harder to understand people if I couldn't see their faces. I couldn't tell if they were happy or sad, joking or serious. What if I misunderstood something and didn't realize until too late? I knew Julie would never laugh at me, but I hated feeling stupid.

This was the first time Julie had said the word "summer" without rolling her eyes or groaning. I was about to raise my eyebrows in a silent question when I felt a poke in my back.

I closed my eyes, breathed deeply and kept walking. Robbie and his friends made weird noises that I guess were supposed to sound like another language, but came out more like barnyard-animal noises instead.

"We can get to work on the plan as soon as we get to my place," Julie said. "Our summers are going to be better than we thought."

Her eyes sparkled, and she looked so excited I could hardly wait to hear what she had in mind.

When Robbie started yelling, "Hey, Rosie, where's your sombrero?" in my ear, I finally lost my patience. I whipped around, which made him run right into me. He stumbled, and I pulled myself up tall (almost exactly his height), crossed my arms over my chest and stared at him.

"Government leech," he shouted. I put my nose right in close against his and stared some more. He twisted up his face and accused me of trying to kiss him, but he also took a step back.

And I took one forward. Uncertainty flashed in his eyes.

"Come on, guys," he said finally. "What's the word for 'crazy' in Spanish? *Loco?* Rosario's *loco*. Let's get outta here."

They went back the way they came, walking with a swagger, and every now and then shouting words like "freak" and "idiot." My English wasn't perfect, but I knew what those words meant.

"At least we're rid of them for now," I said when they turned a corner and couldn't hear me speak.

Julie was laughing. "Don't take this the wrong way, but I think you *are* a bit *loco*. Nobody stands up to Robbie like that."

"*Loca*," I muttered. "He said it wrong. *Loco* is for boys and men, not girls. Robbie and his friends don't even say insults properly."

"Intelligence isn't their strong point," Julie said, linking her arm with mine again. We turned toward her house, the blue one halfway down the block with the big green lawn and the cedar fence.

"Strong point?" I asked as we climbed the front steps.

"Something someone's good at," she explained.

Julie knew more words than any other kid I'd ever met. She seemed happy when I asked her about them, and our teacher was always impressed when I used them in my writing. I think my good writing was another reason Ms. Bower let me be silent in class. She could tell I was learning, no matter how quiet I was.

"Being a good friend is Julie's strong point," I said. "I use it like that?"

Her cheeks turned a bit pink. "Yes," she said, "and thank you."

She opened the door, and the smell of chocolate-chip cookies wafted out to meet us. Julie and her mother, Ms. Norton, had introduced me to cookies a few months earlier. In Mexico we had something similar called *galletitas,* but they were bigger and puffier and usually had coconut or nuts in them.

Now that I was coming over most days after school, Julie's mother made cookies once a week, and sometimes she even packed up some for my parents. That's how the food exchange started between our two families. Our parents couldn't speak each others' languages, but they communicated with cookies, *estofado,* pizza, lasagna and *quesadillas.* I wouldn't have known half as much about Canada if it hadn't been for Julie and her mother. I don't think they would know as much about

Mexico either. Now they are even trying to learn a few words of Spanish.

I took off my shoes at the front door, like Canadians do, and shrugged off my backpack.

"Now let's get to work on the plan," said Julie as she led me down the hall.

CHAPTER 2

Build Your Own Adventure

"You're going to love it!" Julie sat on her bedroom floor, munching on a cookie and sticking one hand deep into her backpack. I leaned back against one wall, nibbling my cookie. Her room had green walls, a green bedspread and a bumpy beige carpet. In the middle of her spotless black desk sat a computer with a big screen, and all around were shelves with enough books for a small library.

She pulled a thin colorful library book from her backpack and slid it across the floor toward me. *How to Make Your Own Book* it said on the cover. I placed my cookie on one leg, brushed the crumbs off my fingers and flipped through the pages. I liked making things myself, and I loved the idea of making books instead of always having to buy them in the store, but I didn't see how this would make our summers any less lonely. Besides, where would I get the pretty paper and thick thread that we'd need? I hated asking my parents for things they couldn't afford.

"Isn't it fantastic?" Julie wanted to know.

I nodded. "The books are pretty. Will you make one this summer?"

"We could each make one," she said. "That's my plan."

She looked like she was waiting for me to stand up and cheer or something, but when I didn't, Julie let out an impatient sigh. "This summer, we could each write a whole book!" she said. "We can make notes on everything that happens to us while we're apart, and then in September, we can write a good copy and add photos and drawings and stuff, and then we can make books and give them to each other so we'll each know exactly what the other person did over the summer." Her face lit up like a firecracker on a Mexican Christmas Eve.

I tried to share her excitement, but I was never any good at lying. "I don't know enough English to write a book," I said.

"Oh, don't worry about the English," she said, passing me the plate of cookies. "I can help you make it perfect at the end, if you want." She wrinkled her forehead, like she was working hard to stay excited. "Don't you want to make your own book?"

"I do," I said quickly. She knew how much I loved writing stories and making things with my hands. She knew that I dreamed of growing up and writing books in English and in Spanish, stories like those that filled the library shelves. I knew I wasn't ready to write a book now though. Even if my English was perfect, what was I going to write about? As soon as I said I did want to write a book, Julie leaped up to pull a new notebook from a stack in her closet. Then she poked around in a desk drawer for a pen, and I was pretty sure she was about to design a plan of action. Julie made plans of action for every project she started, from building a kite to helping her mother make banana bread.

Instead of opening the notebook, Julie handed the book and pen to me. "You're going to need these," she said. "We have to keep notes on all the exciting stuff we do this summer." I held her gift gingerly on my knees and felt embarrassed heat creeping into my cheeks. I thought of giving the book back and telling Julie

I had plenty at home. But of course she'd know I was lying. She knew my parents always bought what I needed for school, but there was no money for extra supplies.

And I knew my parents wouldn't approve of this gift. They didn't believe in charity. Even when the government invited us to come to Canada, paid for our flight and offered to pay all our expenses for a year to help us get settled in our new country, my parents worked as hard as they could to learn English and find jobs so they could start paying for everything themselves before the year was over. They were always talking about honor and how important it is to stand tall and know you can look after yourself.

I didn't want to give the notebook back. With its shiny blue plastic cover and a long wire spiral down one side, it was fancier than anything my parents bought me. Writing in a book like that would make me feel like I *could* write a whole book. Hadn't Ms. Bower said that my writing was "exceptionally insightful" for my age? (I had to look up both words in the dictionary, and then I had to look up the words in the definitions. In the end, I decided it meant I wrote things that most kids didn't think to write about.)

Julie pulled another notebook and pen from her backpack, stretched out on her tummy and held her pen over an empty page. "If we try hard, we'll have lots of stories for our books by the end of the summer. We might even have to make *two* books each!"

I laughed so much that I sprayed cookie crumbs. Julie frowned, and I apologized. "It will be easy for you," I said, opening my book to my own first smooth page. "You'll have an exciting summer in Vancouver. I don't know what I will write about."

She looked up at me, surprised. "But your life is way more interesting than mine," she said. "I'm just hanging out with my dad all summer. You get to go to work with your parents, and pick flowers, and grow vegetables, and do stuff that kids around here never do."

"They don't do it, because they don't have to," I said. Sometimes kids went to the fields to pick flowers or vegetables, but they only went once. I didn't know any other kids who had to work the whole summer with their parents. "What will I write? A story called *How to Grow a Kiwi* or *How to Pull*"—I searched for the word and couldn't find it—"*How to Pull Bad Little Plants from a Garden.*"

"Weeds?" Julie asked.

"The little plants that the farm doesn't want," I said. "Is that weeds?"

She nodded. I took an almost-full notebook from my backpack, flipped it open near the end and asked her to spell the word. Then I wrote it down with its translation in Spanish, *hierbas malas*. I'd remember it that way.

I was going to miss Julie. I didn't have any other friends my age, and since the only person I spoke English with was leaving, I had decided not to speak English at all that summer. I would speak only Spanish with my parents and the other farm workers who had come from Mexico to work on the farm. When I was alone, I would practice my English words to myself, saying them over and over until I said each one like a Canadian. I didn't want to write any of that into my book. I wanted to be a Normal Canadian Kid, with Normal Canadian Kid stories.

"You'll find something good to write about," Julie said. "You'll see. And if you don't find any adventures, you'll just have to make them up." She got a *Eureka!* look on her face and scribbled something in her notebook.

I looked around her room and thought about her summer in the city—going to the park, the pool and maybe even a summer camp. Her summer would be full of Normal Canadian Kid adventures.

Stories about *my* summer would only make me feel weirder than ever. A normal Canadian kid would never write about working in flower fields, or eating beans and rice, or speaking Spanish. What was the point of speaking English perfectly if everything I wrote about was weird anyway? Even with perfect grammar, I couldn't imagine what I could write that anyone— even my best friend—would want to read.

CHAPTER 3

What's Normal?

I got home just as my parents pulled up in their ancient green station wagon. It was secondhand, rusty and twice as old as me. Even here, in the cheapest part of Victoria, no one had a car this old, but my parents were proud of it. We had never been rich enough to own a car in Mexico.

"*Hola, mi amor*," Papá called, climbing out of the front seat. Beside him, Mamá rummaged around on the floor, collecting the bags full of plastic lunch containers.

I ran to Papá and almost knocked him over with my hug. He kissed the top of my head, and I breathed in his smell: plants, sweat and sunshine. To me, that was the smell of happiness, no matter where we were living.

When my parents first started working in Canada, it was winter and so they got indoor jobs. For a while, instead of smelling like fresh earth, they smelled like the bleach they used to clean floors and toilets in office buildings. They were grumpy and pale and didn't smile much, and I was relieved when they found work in the fields in the spring. My parents were happier with suntanned faces and dirt in their hair. "How is my favorite daughter today?" Papá asked in Spanish, pushing me away from him so he could see my face.

"Your *only* daughter is just fine," I said, and he tweaked my nose.

I laughed and ran around to the other side of the car to help Mamá with the bags. It was good to hear my father joke again. He used to make that favorite daughter joke all the time, and he had called my only brother, Ricardo, his favorite son. Ricardo was seventeen when he was killed in Mexico three years ago, and for a long time after that, Papá stopped joking altogether.

Soon after Ricardo died, when I was seven, my parents started whispering to each other in the kitchen of our little house in Mexico. From my bed in the corner,

I heard words like "persecution," "escape," "safe place," and "Guatemala." The first words made sense after Ricardo was killed. No one knew exactly who had killed him, but people talked. They said my brother had been speaking out against the Mexican government, and someone got angry and shot him. They said people might suspect my family of disagreeing with the government too, and we'd better be careful. My parents didn't want me to know any of that, so I pretended not to know…and not to be scared.

But I didn't understand why my parents were talking about Guatemala. The country next to ours was even more dangerous than our part of Mexico. Why would anyone want to escape to *there*?

I stayed awake trying to hear every last word of my parents' whispers, but they still didn't make sense. One day, Papá left the house right after supper, and I followed him to the end of our street. When he stopped in front of *el viejo* Claudio's house, I hid around the corner where I could still hear them. Old Claudio looked a million years old and always sat outside on a stool, talking to passers-by. I had no idea why Papá would want to talk to him, but my father must have whispered a question because *el viejo* looked thoughtful; then he answered in his raspy voice. "It's a tough journey," he said, "and once you arrive, there's no guarantee they'll accept you. You might have to wait for years, and in Guatemala, you'll be worse off than here, *m'hijo*."

My father had his back to me, so I couldn't see the look on his face, but I was smiling. I had been right all along. No matter how scary things were here, my parents couldn't be crazy enough to move to Guatemala.

"But if Canada does accept us," my father said, "they'll pay for our flight there?"

I almost fell out of my hiding place when he asked that. Had he said Canada? That was so far north, it was almost at the end of the map on the wall of our classroom. What did Canada have to do with us? And what was this about flying? Weren't they talking about Guatemala only a second ago? If I hadn't been so worried that my father would discover me eavesdropping, I would have run the three blocks to *Abuela*'s house to tell my grandmother that Papá had gone crazy.

Later, I sometimes wished that he *had* gone crazy. At least there are medicines for craziness. There's no cure for leaving your country, your home and everyone you've ever known. Of course, I never said any of that to my parents. When Papá explained that he wanted to take us to that big country at the end of the map, I didn't say anything at all. He explained that the best way to get to Canada was to go to Guatemala first because the Canadian government had an office there. We would tell the Canadians what had happened to Ricardo and that we were in danger too. "If the Canadians understand why we had to leave Mexico," Papá said, "they'll invite us to their country. Canada sometimes pays for people in danger to go to Canada so they can be safe."

If that was true, then why didn't everyone go to Canada? "What if they don't believe us?" I asked. "Or what if too many people want to go to Canada? What then?"

Papá looked at me, and I saw the fear in his eyes before he could hide it. "I don't know, *m'hija*," he said. "I don't know, but one thing is certain. We can't stay here."

The trip from Mexico to Guatemala was awful. We couldn't carry much food, and we passed through lots of places that were far more dangerous than our town.

Thieves attacked us, and Papá got beaten pretty badly. When we finally made it to noisy, crowded Guatemala City, we were tired, hungry and sick, and still we had to wait for almost a year before we got to talk to the Canadian Embassy. All that time, my parents said again and again that they were doing this for my future. So that I would have a future.

Everyone knows there's no point arguing when adults are talking like that.

"*Qué día*," Mamá said now, getting out of the station wagon. With the fingers of one hand, she ruffled the dirt out of her short black hair. "It's been a long day. *Cómo estás,* Rosario?"

"I'm fine," I said, taking a few of the bags from her hands. She smiled at me, waiting to hear about my day, and I scrambled to find something to tell her. But the only things that came to mind were things I couldn't say—about Robbie or about not talking at school. My parents had no idea I didn't speak to anyone but Julie. They only saw what Ms. Bower wrote on the top of my assignments, and they thought they had a genius daughter. When they had to sign my report cards, I translated for them and left out the parts that urged me to try harder when it came to my speaking skills.

I told myself it didn't matter. By September, I would talk like everyone else, and when I brought home my first report card in grade five, I'd be proud to translate the whole thing. Meanwhile, no way was I going to tell my parents the truth about my life in Canada. I would never admit wishing I were back in Mexico, where people liked me and thought I was smart and funny.

"You're not going to tell us a single thing about your day?" Papá asked. We were inside our little basement suite now. Home, if you wanted to call it that. It was nothing like the warm, colorful house we had in Mexico, or the big bright house we lived in when we first came to Victoria and the government was still paying our bills. Mamá and Papá didn't seem to care. They said this ugly little basement was the best kind of home for us because we were safe, and we paid the rent ourselves.

It was bigger than our house in Mexico, or the shack where we lived in Guatemala. Here we had a full living room, a bedroom for my parents, a separate kitchen and an indoor bathroom with a shower. With a little effort, I could ignore the musty smell, the stained carpet, the naked lightbulbs and the big chunks of floor covering missing in the kitchen. At least we were safe here.

I slept on the couch in the living room. Mamá had hung some sheets from the ceiling so I could have some privacy. My favorite part of the room was the window. If I stood on the back of the couch and leaned up against the wall, I could see out onto the sidewalk and watch people's feet going by. Little feet in shiny black shoes that skipped next to bigger feet in pink sneakers. Or high heels that clicked past as though there was no time to lose. I could imagine whole lives based on shoes and how they moved. And the best part was that no one knew I was watching them, my nose at ground level. Too bad I couldn't write a book about all the things I could imagine about feet, I thought.

And suddenly I had it! The perfect thing to tell my parents about my day! "You'll never guess what Julie and I are going to do this summer. We're going to write books!" I collapsed in a heap on one of the lawn chairs in the corner of the kitchen, relieved to have something positive to tell them.

Mamá deposited her bags on the cracked and yellowed kitchen counter and was about to respond when Papá called out that he was going to take a shower. She called back to him about getting supper ready and then stood in the middle of the kitchen floor as proud as if I'd brought peace to Mexico. "A whole book, *mi amor*? All in English?"

I shrugged, suddenly wishing I'd mentioned something else. I didn't want to get her hopes up. "It was Julie's idea. She'll have lots of things to write about this summer, and in September, we'll turn it into a book, so she suggested I write about my summer too. I think I'll write a very short book." I smiled at her.

Mamá laughed, opened the fridge and pulled out a pot of spicy beans, a few *tortillas* and a tomato. "Oh, Rosario. I'm sure you'll find lots to write about too, and it'll be good to keep working on your English, especially if you're speaking Spanish with us in the fields all day."

"I guess so," I said, "but tell me about your day. Did you see José? Has he talked to Analía this week yet?"

Mamá laughed again and handed me a tomato to chop. "You've made a good friend in him, haven't you?" she asked. "I don't think he'll be talking to his family until Friday night, so I don't have any new Analía stories for you."

"That's okay," I said. "I'll get to hear them all on Saturday when we go to the fields with Julie and her mother. I can't believe Julie hasn't met José yet.

Isn't that funny? I can't imagine Canada without either one of them, and they don't even know each other!"

Mamá told me about her day on the farm, mostly weeding between hundreds of cabbages. When Papá came in, she asked me to watch the *tortillas* sizzling in the pan while she showered.

Papá patted his wet hair into place and smoothed his at-home jeans, the clean pair that he never wore to the fields. "What did you dream about today?" he asked, as he often did. Where Mamá was practical and always wanted to know what had happened, Papá wanted to know what I wished *would* happen. Sometimes that made him a lot easier to talk to.

But not today. How could I tell him I dreamed we were back in Mexico, or that my brother was still alive and would come to school and tell Robbie to watch out? (I often wondered what Ricardo would think of Canada, but if he were still alive, we probably wouldn't be here.) How could I say I wished we had enough money for me to go to summer camp, or that I wished Julie didn't have to go away?

"I dreamed that we didn't have a math test tomorrow," I said finally, "and a spelling test the day after. What about you?"

Papá grabbed a flipper and turned over the blackened *tortilla* I had totally forgotten about. "I dreamed that we could travel across the whole province," he said. "Just pack up the station wagon and go. A few of the men at work have been all the way across, and they said there's plenty to see. Did you know there's even a desert, with cactuses and everything?"

"Really?" I asked. "Like in Mexico?"

"*Sí, señorita*! And there are huge lakes, two sets of gigantic mountains, little towns, moose and deer and even bears, all the way along. Now *that* would be an amazing summer. One day, when we have the money..."

One day, I thought. Always one day. It was going to be a long time before I ever had a Normal Canadian Kid story to write.

CHAPTER 4

Field Trip

Julie spent Saturdays watching cartoons, going to the library and playing games on her computer. Other kids talked about soccer games, movies or going to the mall. I never did those things on Saturdays, but I wouldn't have traded my Saturdays for anything.

This particular Saturday in May was going to be the best one yet because Julie and her mother, Ms. Norton, were coming with us to the tulip farm.

"What an experience this will be!" Ms. Norton stood in the early morning light beside our station wagon, rubbing her arms and stamping her feet in the cold. Julie's eyes were still half-closed behind her glasses, and her thin blond hair was tied in a stick-out-everywhere ponytail. She didn't look happy about being there, and for a moment, I wondered if it was a mistake to take them along.

Our friendship so far had taken place at school and at her house, speaking English, talking about Canadian things and eating Canadian food (with a few Mexican things sent along from Mamá). Sure, I'd told her about our lives in Mexico and how we escaped to Guatemala, and she'd always seemed interested. Now, though, as I saw her frowning, squinting face, a little knot formed in my stomach. What if she didn't like the tulip fields? What if the rows and rows of yellow, red, white, purple and orange didn't make her happy like they made me, and what if she didn't like the rich, damp smell of fresh-turned soil?

"We'll finally see how flowers get from the field to our dining-room table," said Ms. Norton, putting enough music into her voice to make up for Julie's grumpy silence. "I bet we'll have a whole new appreciation for farmers and farming after today, right, honey?"

Julie rubbed her eyes and stifled a yawn. "Mum loves learning experiences," she said to me, "even at five thirty on a Saturday morning." The corners of her lips turned up, and the knot in my stomach loosened a little.

Ms. Norton laughed, and Mamá smiled. It was funny to see the two mothers together: tall and short, well-dressed and shabby, light-skinned and dark, excited and nervous. They'd never have met if Julie and I weren't friends. And we became friends only because we were the last ones to find partners for the spring social-studies project.

Mamá's eyes darted to meet mine, and I could tell she didn't understand why Ms. Norton was laughing or whether she should join in. I translated into Spanish what Ms. Norton and Julie had said, and Mamá laughed for real. Sometimes I wished I could take all the English I'd learned and drop it into my parents' heads. They spoke a bit but didn't understand much, and they didn't have time to go to any more English classes. I'd tried to teach them, but they never got better, always saying it was easier for kids to learn new languages. As if it was easy for me.

Papá threw an extra bottle of water into the trunk and banged it shut. "Are ready to go," he said carefully, not meeting Ms. Norton's eyes. I felt my face flushing with embarrassment at his bad English, and at the same time, I was ready to tell off anyone who corrected him. Usually, if they had to communicate in English, my parents used their hands a lot. With Julie's mother though, they made a special effort. And Ms. Norton seemed to understand how hard they were trying, even if the English words didn't come out very well. Ms. Norton and Julie even tried out their few words of Spanish sometimes. They'd got language CDs out of the library and liked to talk to us about the weather.

"You see here." Mamá offered Ms. Norton the seat next to Papá. Julie's mother nodded thank-you and slipped into the front seat. Julie, Mamá and I piled into the back.

And we were off, windows down, racing along the still-empty streets toward the highway, past the subdivisions and the billboards with huge pictures of hotels, happy people and restaurant dinners.

"Fantastic!" Julie shouted into the wind when the tulip fields burst into view. "I've never seen so much color."

I grinned. It looked like today was going to be a great day after all.

"Maybe you no like it so much after," Papá said. "Maybe too tired."

Ms. Norton talked about what hard work farming was. I don't know if my parents understood much of what she said, but I was grateful for the talk. It made us seem like a normal group of friends, going on a field trip. Julie caught my eye and made a fish face, and we both laughed.

I hoped Papá was wrong. I hoped Julie and her mother would love the fields so much they'd want to come back every Saturday. For a wild moment, I even imagined Julie canceling her summer in Vancouver... but of course that was impossible. Why would she give up a summer with her father in a skyscraper, going to summer camp and playing at the beach to work in a field? If I were her, I would never give those things up. Not that I would ever have the chance.

CHAPTER 5

Tulips

"*Hola, m'hija!*" José called when the five of us made our way into the field. He was trailing behind the pickers, collecting their bundles of flowers into a plastic tray. He set down his tray at the end of a row and waved.

I waved back, grabbed Julie's hand and ran toward him—*thlop, thlop, thlop*—in my too-big rubber boots.

Julie's boots made strange noises as she ran too, and she laughed as she tried to keep up. "Where are we going?" she asked. "Is that José? The one who lives in a hotel and whose family is in Mexico?"

"Yes! He is the one I toll you about." I was talking too fast to correct my mistake. Told, I reminded myself, with a *d*.

We hurried along to where José stood. I thought it was funny that Julie remembered about the hotel and his family in Mexico because those details described almost all of the workers on the farm. José and the other workers weren't political refugees like us, so they weren't allowed to stay in Canada forever. They could only stay here during farming season. The farmer here put them up in a hotel while they were in Canada, and they were only allowed to come to Canada *because* they had family in Mexico and would want to go back.

"*Tu amiga?*" José asked when we reached him.

"Yes," I answered in Spanish. "This is my friend Julie. Remember I told you about her?"

José bowed like Julie was a queen, and he let his grin do the talking for him.

"He doesn't speak much English," I told Julie.

She frowned. "But hasn't he been here for a long time already?"

"Eight months last year, and three months this year. On the farm, though, he speaks only Spanish with the other workers," I said. "They all work as many days as they can, so they can take back as much money as possible to their families in Mexico. There's no time to learn English."

"Oh," Julie said, pushing her glasses back up her nose. She gave José a shy smile but said nothing, which surprised me. I'd told her a million times that José was one of those grown-ups who think kids have interesting things to say and plenty of good ideas, and Julie always wanted to know more about Mexico.

"You can talk to him, you know," I said. "I can translate."

She nodded and her eyebrows pulled together, as though she was trying to think of the perfect question.

"Pick?" José asked, pointing to the rows of tulips beginning at our feet and stretching out to the top of the hillside. Julie grinned, and we both nodded. José bent over and put one hand to his back; then he wiped the back of the other hand across his forehead. "Much work," he said.

Julie pointed to herself and then made a pillow with her hands and pretended to sleep. She pointed to the ground at the end of one of the tulip rows, and José laughed.

They liked each other. Just as I'd hoped they would.

My parents and Ms. Norton caught up to us. Julie's mother had swapped her white runners for pink rubber boots. I introduced José, who held out his hand, then blushed when he saw it was covered in dirt. He wiped it on his pants, but in the end, the adults only smiled at each other.

I was about to step into one of the rows of flowers when I remembered something. "Hey, José," I said. "Can I show Julie your picture of Analía? I always tell her Analía's stories, and she wants to know what your daughter looks like."

Analía was ten years old, just like Julie and me, and she lived in Mexico City with her mother, brothers and sisters. I loved listening to José's stories about her. A few weeks earlier, her detective club had discovered who'd been leaving boxes of fresh *tortillas* at the end of her street, enough for each house in the whole block. (It was a church group from a rich part of the city.) Another time, she and a friend rescued a puppy from a ditch, nursed it back to health and named it Fred because José had told her that *Pedro Picapiedra* is called Fred Flintstone in English.

José handed Julie a picture in a plastic cover. A girl our age with a blue flower in her long black hair smiled up at us. She looked like she'd be as good at telling jokes as her father was.

Above our heads, the adults kept talking. "Have you heard about the barbecue?" José asked Papá. "A bunch of us are organizing one this Sunday to celebrate the warm weather." He chuckled and shook his head. "Can you believe it? It's finally getting warm enough to pick without a jacket, and it's time for us to leave! Of all the rotten luck."

I looked up, confused. "Time to leave? But you just got here, didn't you? I thought you were staying until the fall."

José crouched down so his face was level with mine. "I wish we could," he said. "Some years, we get to stay in one place for a whole season, or even two. But other times, we have to move around a lot. Pretty soon, we're going to the mainland to a place called Oliver to pick cherries and peaches. We'll really be seeing the province this summer!"

He tried to smile, but his eyes were sad, and when I looked at my parents, they too had fake smiles on their faces. I frowned at all of them. Why was everyone pretending to be happy with this terrible news? If the other Mexican workers left the farm, Mamá and Papá wouldn't have anyone to talk to. They'd come home exhausted and cranky. This summer was looking worse and worse. Too upset to think up anything new to say, I translated for Julie.

She didn't say anything, and I could tell she didn't understand how awful this news was.

All day, I tried not to think about José leaving. I tried to have fun with Julie and to concentrate on slicing the tulips from their bulbs and making perfect bundles. Julie tried hard too. She taught me how to play *veo veo* in English, a game Ricardo used to play with me when I was small. Soon I learned the English words by heart. "I spy with my little eye, someting that is...blue."

"Some*th*ing," Julie said gently. "Not some*t*ing."

"I know, I know," I said. "Some*th*ing. You guess now!"

We soon passed Ms. Norton, who was picking in the next row, close to Mamá who was trying to explain about staying close to the ground.

"No too much stand," Mamá said. "Like dees."

Ms. Norton smiled and shook her head. "I can't believe how fast you pick," she said, "and how you can hold so many bundles at the same time." She tried to imitate Mamá—one bundle in her right hand, one under her left arm, and three between the fingers of her left hand—and they all fell to the ground like spilled matches. "I won't even earn enough money for an ice-cream cone, the way I'm going," Ms. Norton said, but she didn't seem too upset.

"Eees okay," Mamá said. "You learn."

By lunchtime, Ms. Norton said she was exhausted and couldn't imagine how anyone could work like this six days a week. She and Julie stayed for the rest of the day and picked 150 bundles. "That'll cover the ice cream," Ms. Norton joked when she got her cash at the end of the day. "It might even be enough for double scoops."

We all piled into the car, headed back into town and stopped at a little ice-cream shop by the water, halfway between the Parliament buildings and the blue bridge. I ordered rocky road and mango. Julie had lemon and vanilla. If I didn't think about José and Julie leaving and just how lonely this summer was going to be, I could consider it a good day.

When we got home, Mamá wanted to open the week's mail, which meant I had to pull out the dictionary and help my parents read difficult English sentences, mostly about buying magazines or newspapers, or signing up for credit cards.

One of the letters, though, didn't offer us anything at all.

In fact, it took everything away.

CHAPTER 6

My Wonderful, Impossible Plan

"We must move away!" I told Julie on Monday morning, as soon as she opened her front door. The smile fell from her face, and she stopped pulling on her backpack and stared at me. I tried to swallow the lump in my throat. "The owner of the house sent to my parents a letter. He wants us to pay more for rent, I tink—I looked up the biggest words in the dictionary. But we cannot pay more. My parents said now we must find anodder apartment." My words tumbled out before I could check them for mistakes, and I was too upset to care about anything but where on earth we were going to live.

"Oh," Julie said, pushing up her glasses, twice. She stood there with one shoe on and the other off, her backpack hanging from one shoulder. "But you won't move very far, right? I mean, you won't move away from Victoria, will you?"

"I don't know," I said. "My parents want to move closer to the farm, but I don't want to. Now dere is not enough work for José and some of de other Mexicans. So maybe later dere will not be enough work for my parents. I don' want to live far away with no work!" The words flew out of my mouth, mistake after mistake piling up before I could even sort out what I was going to say next.

Julie was ignoring the mistakes. We stood in silence for a few minutes. "If you're near the farm, I could still visit you, right?" she whispered. "I mean it's not the other end of the province or anything."

She looked as miserable as I felt, but at least one person in Canada cared where we moved. One person in the entire country. When we left Mexico, half the town turned up at our doorstep the night before, with cookies and *tortillas*, pictures of saints, lucky charms, photographs and even a Bible to bring along on our journey. Almost a year later, when we left Guatemala to come to Canada, everyone on our street threw a party for us. Now we had chosen to stay in Canada forever.

We had been here for close to a year, and only one person would be sad to see us leave the neighborhood. Sometimes, I thought, no matter how much you want a place to be home, it simply doesn't feel like it.

And that's when I thought of the plan. The wonderful, impossible plan. I wasn't going to say a thing about it yet. Not to Julie anyway. We walked to school, talking about the math test instead, and when we saw the other kids, I went quiet as usual, and she told me about her latest notes for her summer adventures. She didn't sound very excited anymore.

In class, I made a few notes of my own in the notebook Julie had given me, but I wasn't writing about what I'd do this summer. I was writing about how to get my parents to agree to my wonderful, impossible plan. With Julie *and* José leaving, I had nothing to lose. Anywhere would be better than here for the summer.

As soon as Papá and Mamá got home that afternoon, I asked them what they thought.

"It's too risky," Papá said. "Too much to plan in too little time. Too many things could go wrong." He was sitting at the kitchen table with his arms crossed. Mamá was leaning back in her chair, looking exhausted. The empty supper plates sat waiting to be washed.

I took a deep breath and was about to try again when Mamá said, "I agree with your father. We can't just travel across the province right now, following the harvests like the other Mexicans. They *have* to do it because they signed a contract, and that's why they're here in Canada, but it's different for us. Our home is here. We can't just pack it all away and leave it behind."

"But why not?" I asked. Would Ricardo have backed me up if he were still alive? He used to do that sometimes, sticking up for me when he knew I wanted something really badly. Even though we didn't always get along—he was so much older than me and we didn't have much in common—I missed him now. "It would only be for a couple of months," I said, "and it's perfect timing. I won't be in school in the summer, so I can help in the fields, like I do on Saturdays. And Papá's been talking about exploring the province ever since we got here. And we have a car, and you two are really good at harvesting, and José said that farmers are desperate for help. Besides, imagine how much money José must be making if he can afford to fly back and forth to Mexico every summer!"

For some reason, they smiled at that, but they still didn't look convinced. "José doesn't pay for those flights, Rosario," Papá said. "The farmers do."

I frowned. That didn't make any sense. "Why would they do that?"

"Because the farmers need people to harvest their flowers and fruit," said Mamá. "And Mexican workers need money to survive. It's hard to find work in Mexico, and people would rather leave their families behind and put food on the table than let them starve."

"But lots of Canadians need jobs too," I said. "Why don't the farmers hire them instead of paying for all those flights?"

"Because most Canadians don't want to work so hard for so little money," Papá said, pushing back from the table. "Getting up at five and working bent over for twelve hours a day. Most Canadians would demand higher wages if they had to work like that. But that's not what we were talking about. We were talking about why we can't just leave our lives behind and follow the harvests."

Mamá began clearing the dishes, and she motioned for me to help, as if the conversation was already over. I grabbed the knives and forks from the table and dropped them with a clatter onto the plates. Mamá ran water in the sink, and Papá stayed in his seat because, with two other people moving around in the tiny kitchen, he had no room to get up. He stared at the vinyl tabletop as though it might solve all our problems.

"It's not so easy," Mamá said as she scrubbed. "First of all, we would need to find a place for all of our things. That costs money. Gas for traveling costs money, and where would we stay while we're on the farms? José and the others always have somewhere to stay because the farms give housing to foreign workers, but we would have to find our own spot. That would take time *and* money, and so we'd still be no better off than we are here."

"But it doesn't have to be that way," I said, snatching a frayed pink dishtowel from a hook at the edge of the counter. "Julie's family has a big tent that they haven't used in years. Ms. Norton said that we could borrow it whenever we want to. She said there are campsites all over British Columbia, and some only cost a dollar a night. That's much less than rent. And the other great thing is that Julie has a big basement with plenty of space in it. We don't have much stuff, and I'm sure they'd let us keep it there if we asked."

I'd written all this stuff in my notebook that day, and I was ready for any excuse my parents could think up. Ricardo would have been proud of me. No matter what, I was going to win this discussion. It was my only shot at a summer with enough Normal Canadian Kid stories for my book. If I wrote about all the places we camped, I wouldn't even have to mention that I worked with my parents during the day.

Our few pieces of furniture and our winter clothes wouldn't take up much space in Julie's basement, and best of all, if our things were at her place, we'd have to come back here to live instead of going somewhere else. I wouldn't have to start all over again at a whole new school that might have even more Robbie Zecs than this one, and I wouldn't have to leave behind my only friend in the whole country.

My parents looked at each other. They weren't disagreeing with me anymore, so I kept talking as fast as I could. "We could travel all the way across, just like you said, Papá. First strawberries and raspberries in the Fraser Valley. Later cherries and peaches on the edge of the desert. We'll meet all sorts of people and see a million places, and I'll help you in the fields every day, and after peaches, we'll be rich! And we can come back here and choose any apartment we want. Maybe even one in the big buildings downtown, with a pool, or a garden on the roof!"

At last they smiled. Mamá even laughed. "I think," she said, "we'd have to invest in some new furniture if we wanted one of those fancy apartments. They wouldn't want lawn chairs in their kitchens and children sleeping on sofas."

She was teasing, of course—and changing the subject—but she looked less worried than she had since we got that letter about the rent going up.

"So you'll think about it?" I asked.

Papá sighed. "I don't know," he said. "A lot depends on the charity of Julie's mother…"

I bit my tongue and shook out my towel in a noisy *thwap*. I knew they hated accepting charity, but I also knew that they really liked Ms. Norton, and that she'd be more than happy to help.

"We'll think about it," Papá said finally, and I tossed my towel onto the counter and bounded across the kitchen to hug him.

CHAPTER 7

Strawberries

After that, I spent every spare moment researching farms on the Internet, helping my mother pack or learning to set up the big green tent in Julie's backyard. Ms. Norton not only offered her tent and storage space in her basement, she also e-mailed each farm that we thought of visiting. "To make sure it's okay for you to work, Rosario," she said. "In Canada, kids have to be twelve years old to work, even with their parents' permission, but hopefully it'll be okay for you to help your parents while *they're* working."

Thank goodness Ms. Norton knew these things. In our town in Mexico, everyone worked because otherwise families couldn't make enough money to buy food. Canada had more rules than I'd ever imagined.

Luckily the farms wrote back to say children were welcome. "As long as parents look after them and they don't eat all the fruit," Ms. Norton added, giving me a pretend-serious look.

I have no idea why my parents eventually agreed to my wonderful, impossible plan. Maybe they liked the idea of not paying rent for two months, or maybe they were as curious as I was about seeing the rest of the province. I didn't ask questions. I wanted to get on the road before they changed their minds again.

The night before we left, Julie gave me a little white box. "So you don't have any excuses not to write," she said. When I opened it, I found a battery-operated light to clip onto my notebook when it was dark out.

I threw my arms around her, and suddenly I missed her, even though we hadn't left yet. When I left my friends in Mexico and Guatemala, I knew I might never see them again. I'd never had a chance to say good-bye to my brother. I knew this time everything was supposed to be different. The whole idea was to come back here in September with more money and a whole summer of adventures behind us. If there was one thing I'd learned though, it was that you could never know exactly what was going to happen.

So I said good-bye to Julie as though I'd never see her again. She hugged me right back, and Ms. Norton gave us a bag full of chocolate-chip cookies for our trip.

Early the next morning, our car was stuffed with everything we'd need for our summer adventure: a tent, sleeping bags, a cooler, cutlery and all sorts of other things my parents thought might come in handy. Maybe they were making up for how little we took when we left Mexico for Guatemala, and Guatemala for Canada. It was a wonder the old station wagon could move with all the stuff we'd crammed in.

We took the first ferry of the day from Vancouver Island to the rest of Canada. Mamá and Papá and I sat outside on the upper deck, watching the seagulls above the ship and the sunlight sparkling on the water. Later, our car rumbled off the ferry with a long line of other cars, and we drove along big highways with farms or trees on either side. After what seemed like forever, we turned onto a smaller road and finally came to a stop in a gravel parking lot with a floppy-headed scarecrow and a big wooden sign that said *Green's Farm— Strawberry Capital of the Fraser Valley.*

"We're here!" I shouted from the backseat.

"*Vamonos!* Let's go!" Mamá smiled at me in the rearview mirror. "We've got berries to pick!"

I was out of the car in an instant. The farm was exactly like the photo I'd seen on the website. In the last month, Julie and I had spent hours at her computer, looking for farms, and later I brought Mamá and Papá to the computers at the library to show them what we'd found. Beyond the edge of the parking lot, little green strawberry plants stretched far into the distance, all the way to the edge of the forest.

Two teenagers stood by stacks of white plastic buckets at the entrance to the field. "We pay thirty-five cents a pound," said the one with pimples and glasses. "Leave the buckets at the end of the row, and we'll weigh them on your way out. Make sure you get red berries with a bit of the stem on. Not green. Not brown. Red."

I held my breath and looked at my parents to see if they understood. They didn't know about my decision not to speak English this summer, and they wouldn't understand it if I told them. Sometimes, when they tried their own English with strangers, people talked to them like they were stupid or deaf. When I spoke English though, adults didn't make fun of me the way kids did, so my parents thought my English was perfect. They were so proud to have a daughter who spoke two languages that I never told them the truth.

I was happy my parents didn't have any questions about the strawberries. I nodded to the teenagers and took a few buckets. We headed into the fields, following the dirt road to the far rows. I'd never picked strawberries before, but I loved eating them, and that was why I'd wanted to come to the strawberry farm. I knew we weren't supposed to eat what we picked, but a bite or two wouldn't hurt anyone, I thought.

"On your mark," said Papá.

"Get set," added Mamá.

"Go!" I said, and we each jumped into a row and began picking as fast as we could. We weren't getting paid by the hour here. We'd be paid for each pound of berries we picked. If we wanted to make enough money for a good apartment in the fall, we'd have to pick fast.

The strawberries hung heavy and low against big green leaves, and many hid deep inside the plant. Some of the berries were as wide as my little finger was long. Others were still tiny. But every one I tried was sweet. It was going to be a delicious summer.

I glanced up at my parents. They'd been excited about strawberries too, and for weeks we'd been thinking about this first day of picking. I popped another berry in my mouth. Overhead, an eagle soared and landed in one of the trees at the edge of the field. A girl about my age was picking in the next row over, wearing purple shorts, a purple T-shirt and a purple ribbon in her black hair. Her skin was even darker than mine, and I wondered if she was from another country too. The thing about Canada was that lots of people looked like they came from somewhere else, but they were born here and spoke perfect Canadian English.

Farther along the girl's row, an old woman crouched, picking in fast graceful movements as if her hands were dancing. Her white hair was so long and thick that she'd twisted it up in an enormous bun at the back of her head. And most amazing of all, instead of a shirt, she wore a long piece of green fabric wrapped around her, with a stripe of skin showing at her waist. The green was bright, like new grass, against the darker green of the trees.

They were definitely from far away, I decided. And that made me feel better, somehow. We wouldn't speak, but we'd work here together. We'd look out for each other, without words—like Julie and I did, right at the beginning, when I couldn't say much.

"You're new here, aren't you?" The girl's perfect English interrupted my thoughts, and I couldn't help letting out a disappointed sigh as the image of our silent friendship turned to dust.

I wasn't going to talk to her. She seemed friendly enough, but what if she didn't understand me? Julie kept saying my English was almost perfect, but maybe she was just used to the way I talked.

The girl stared at me. By now I'd taken so long to answer her question that I must have seemed really stupid. I focused on my strawberries. She shrugged and turned away.

I should have felt relieved. After all, I'd saved myself from being embarrassed by my mistakes. Instead I felt sad, and I missed Julie more than ever. The summer stretched out ahead of me, long and lonely.

CHAPTER 8

Analía's Letter

The girl in purple was the only worker who talked to us all day. Most of the others were older women and men, many of them dressed in long pieces of brightly colored fabric. We didn't hear anyone speaking Spanish, but many spoke another language that Mamá thought might be from India.

At the end of the day, the teenagers weighed our buckets, gave Papá a pile of bills and coins, and said the farm opened again at seven o'clock the next morning.

"I'm tired," I said as we crunched across the gravel parking lot. "How much did we make?"

Papá laughed and hugged my shoulders. "Don't you worry about that, *mi amor*," he said. "*Hicimos suficiente*. We made enough, and that's all that matters."

"This summer is about adventure," Mamá agreed, "not money." They seemed so eager to convince me that I wondered if we hadn't made much at all. The next day, I would spend less time looking at the other people in the field and concentrate harder on picking. After all, it was because of me that we were here, and we had to think about finding a better apartment in September.

We piled into the car, which was still crammed with all our camping things, and even though it was only six in the evening, I fell asleep.

"I found it!" Papá called out from the station wagon.

Mamá and I were setting up the tent, its back to the wide, slow Fraser River. Papá was supposed to be getting the sleeping bags out of the car, but instead he was marching toward us, proudly waving a tiny folded rectangle of paper.

"It's about time," said Mamá, and I assumed she was talking about him helping us until she added, "Where was it?"

"What is it?" I asked. I was crouched at one corner of the tent with a peg in my hand. The hard-packed ground was nothing like the soft earth of Julie's lawn, and no amount of banging would get the peg in.

"It slid under the seat," Papá said. "*Para tí*, Rosario, from Analía."

That's weird, I thought, but I was happy for the excuse to stop pounding the tent peg. "Why would José's daughter write to me?"

"I don't know," Papá said. "She told José she wanted to e-mail you. Apparently there's an Internet café close to her school. But José doesn't know anything about the Internet, and he didn't have your e-mail address, so Analía wrote to you the old-fashioned way. This came with one of her family's letters to José." He handed me the note. It was covered with Spanish words, front and back: *For Rosario's eyes only,* Analía wrote. *Do not open unless you are Rosario Ramirez, age 10.*

"José gave it to us the day before he left for the cherry farm," Papá says, looking embarrassed. "We didn't tell you because I lost it almost as soon as he gave it to me. I only found it now when I was looking for the sleeping bags."

"But why would she write to me?" I asked again. I loved hearing stories about Analía, but even my own cousins didn't write to me. It's true that our town in Mexico didn't have Internet like most places in Canada did, and regular mail often got lost on the way to and from the town, but still I always hoped someone would write.

"She wanted a pen pal, I guess," said Mamá. "Pound in the tent peg in your corner, Rosario, *por favor*. The wind's picking up." As soon as she said it, the wind flipped up the far end of the tent, and it bopped Mamá on the head.

She looked so shocked that I couldn't help laughing. Papá and I raced to stop our summer home from flying away.

It wasn't until hours later, when we'd had our supper, the last dish was dried and stacked, and my parents were playing cards at the picnic table, that I pulled the letter from my pocket. With just enough light left in the sky to read by, I sank into the folding chair by the fire pit and smoothed open the paper. Analía's printing was tiny and careful. I felt a flutter of excitement about reading a letter in Spanish. A letter I wouldn't need a dictionary for.

Dear Rosario,

I hope you are as nice as my father says you are. I hope you are happy to get my letter and that you don't think I'm weird for writing to someone I've never met. I <u>feel</u> as if I know you because Papá talks about you every week.

Wow! While I was listening to Analía stories and telling them to Julie, Analía was listening to Rosario stories and maybe telling them to *her* friends. A silly grin spread over my face.

The next line of the letter was mostly scribbled out, but I could still read some of the words.

Sometimes…my father knows…than he does about his own kids!…silly to talk…doesn't <u>choose</u> to work so far away…to send five kids to school.

No wonder she scribbled most of that one out. I tried to ignore it, telling myself it wasn't my fault that I saw more of José than his own daughter did, but it bothered me.

After the scribbling out, Analía wrote, *Oops. Sorry.* That made me smile. I did the same thing when I made a mess of my writing.

Anyway, I wrote to ask you a favor, but please don't tell my father. I'm not supposed to know anything about this, but I overheard my mother tell my aunt, and I figured that if anyone could help him, you could.

I know Papá doesn't want to leave the flower fields to work on the cherry farm. He's heard that the cherry farmer expects people to work too many hours, and he puts a big dog next to the front gate so no one can leave in the evenings. Sometimes people have to sneak out and walk an hour into town if they want to call their families during the week. The workers are only <u>allowed</u> to leave the farm on Sunday afternoons to buy groceries. That's what Papá's heard, anyway. My aunt told Mamá that you can't believe everything you hear, but she's still worried, and so am I.

I put down the letter. This couldn't be right. On the flower farm, José and his friends were allowed to go wherever they wanted after work, just like anyone else. Mostly, they were too tired to do much of anything, but sometimes they went into Victoria to shop or to walk along the waterfront.

Maybe Analía was getting Jose's situation mixed up with something else. I'd heard that farm workers in the United States often had problems with farmers. Papá said many farm workers there weren't really supposed to be in the United States though, and they were so afraid of getting caught by the police that they didn't complain when the farmers treated them badly. I knew it was different in Canada. The Canadian government had *invited* José and the others to help with the Canadian harvest. The farmers gave them a nice place to live and enough work, but not too much, and of course, the farm workers had the same rights as anyone else.

The worst part is that Papá can't change jobs. That's what Mamá told my aunt. She said that those are the rules for Mexican farm workers in Canada: they have to work where they're sent, and if they don't like it, they either put up with it, or they go home. We know Papá would never come home early because our family needs money for food.

We don't know if he'll be able to call us from where he's going. I don't know how far the cherry farm is from the flower fields, but maybe you or someone you know could go there and make sure he's really okay? I know he would tell us on the phone that he's fine, but I want to know for sure. He'd hate to know that I'm asking this, so please don't tell anyone. We only want to know he's all right. Please say you'll help.

Your friend,
Analía.

At the picnic table, my parents were still playing cards. The sun was setting behind the trees, and somewhere a gull cried. I wondered how much my parents knew about the farm where José was now. They had the address, but what else had they heard? I frowned down at the letter. Analía must be confused.

I got up from my folding chair and went to the picnic table. Papá smiled at me, but Mamá was concentrating on her cards. Finally, she slammed down one of them, grinned at my father and stretched. "Another game for me," she said.

Papá rolled his eyes. "Oh well. It's been a good day otherwise." He winked at me.

"Do you like Green's Farm?" I asked, though I hadn't planned to.

"It's okay, I suppose," Papá said. "Plenty of work."

"And I like the smell of strawberries," said Mamá. "How come?"

"It's different from what I expected," I said. "I thought we'd meet more Mexicans." I hoped that didn't sound whiny. Above all, my parents hated complaining. "I mean, I remember you saying that most Canadians don't want to work on farms. I thought there'd be lots of Mexicans."

Mamá put an arm around my shoulders. "It must be tough to spend all day working with no one to talk to but us."

"Kind of," I said.

"I wish I could talk to the other workers too," Papá said. "They'd probably have interesting stories to tell."

"About what?" I asked.

"I wonder if anyone on the farm today knew people in the crash," Mamá said. "It happened near here, didn't it?"

"What crash?" I asked.

"It happened a few months ago," Papá said. "A van full of farm workers crashed near here, and it was all over the news. At work, it was all we talked about for a few weeks because some of the men understood the news reports and said people were starting to worry about how farm workers were treated here."

The words were like an ice cube down my back. We were supposed to be safe here in Canada. No one was supposed to get killed for what they said. Not like Ricardo. "Did someone crash the van on purpose?" I whispered.

Papá shook his head. "No, no. Nothing like that, but the driver wasn't being careful, and she had taken all but two of the seats out of the van so that she could cram more farm workers in. The van only had two seatbelts, and because of that, three people died."

"Oh," I said.

"And then some farm workers started talking about other bad things that happened where they worked," Mamá said. "Lots of dangerous things can happen on a farm, and if workers are new to Canada and don't speak English well, they don't know how to complain. Or who to complain to."

I felt sick. After reading Analía's letter, this was the last thing I wanted to hear.

Papá sighed. "We've been lucky, Rosario, but not everyone is. And many farm workers don't know about the laws that protect us."

"Or if they do know," Mamá added, "they're afraid to complain because they think they might lose their jobs, and they need the money to survive."

"But these things aren't supposed to happen in Canada!" I spluttered. "If there are laws—"

Papá reached across the table to put his hand on mine. "I know, *mi amor*, but people don't always pay attention to the laws. We know that." He got a sad look in his eyes, and I knew he was thinking of my brother.

If people obeyed laws, Ricardo would be alive. My family would never have been in danger, and we never would have had to leave Mexico.

"Don't worry about Green's Farm, Rosario," Mamá said. "I think we'll be okay there. I didn't see anything dangerous, and we've got our own car. Besides, the good thing about working from day to day is that we can always leave if we don't like a place."

I nodded but felt my eyes prick with tears. I blinked them back and told my parents I was going to bed.

It took me forever to get to sleep. Mamá and Papá snored quietly beside me, and I could hear the river lapping against the shore. The wind played between the branches of the trees, and every now and then, on the other side of the campground, the door of the outhouse banged.

Somewhere, across the province, José was trying to sleep too. Was he hungry? Sad? Sick? He'd always been the happiest person in the flower fields, cracking jokes and telling stories. Now I pictured him behind a big chain-link fence, miserable and wishing he were anywhere else.

Analía thought I was smart enough to help him. But how was I supposed to get to the cherry farm without telling anyone why I wanted to go? Papá and Mamá would think I was crazy if I hurried them toward cherries when I had been so excited about strawberries and raspberries. And if José *wasn't* okay, what could I do to change anything?

By the time my eyes finally drifted shut, I still didn't know how to get to the cherry farm, or what I could do once I was there.

That night I dreamed of leaving our town in Mexico. I dreamed of the thieves who stole all our stuff and hit Papá so hard that he fell down, and Mamá and I thought he was dead. And I dreamed of the woman who came running from her house, cleaned his cuts, let us sleep inside and gave us a bag of *tortillas* to take along for our journey the next day. Her kindness didn't bring our stuff back, or heal Papá's black eye and cuts, but we felt less alone because she was there, and that kept us going.

When I woke up, I knew I had to convince my parents that we needed to get to the cherry farm. We had no time to spare.

CHAPTER 9

True or False?

It seemed like we spent a million years picking strawberries. The girl in purple never came back, and no one else talked to us all week. I tried to distract myself by working out something interesting to write about, but so far nothing had happened that I felt like writing down.

I practiced English words to myself as I dropped strawberries into my white bucket, repeating all the words I could think of that had vowels we didn't have in Spanish. When I first started learning English, *bear* and *bird*, *hip* and *heap*, or *collar* and *color* all sounded the same. Between the rows of the strawberry fields, I practiced all of them until each word sounded different, and I thought I sounded Canadian.

Then I tried to imagine what Julie was doing at her father's place—swimming in a pool on top of his skyscraper, or picnicking with him in a park (or, more likely, playing games on her computer or hanging out at the library). I wondered if she and her father would go to the museum she had told me about with the huge movie screen that wrapped around the audience like a giant bubble. Or maybe today they were at the kite store she had mentioned, or walking around the seawall. I invented all sorts of exciting things that Julie might be doing, but no matter what, José and his family kept sneaking into my thoughts.

I'd tried six times to write a letter to Analía, but each letter looked like a list of excuses or a bunch of promises I couldn't keep. In the end, I decided to wait until I could tell her that José was okay. Once we got to the cherry farm, I'd ask José for Analía's e-mail address, find a library or café with Internet access and write to her myself to tell her how things were.

Even after a week of thinking, though, I still didn't know how to make my parents quit strawberry picking and drive east without telling them Analía's suspicions.

One Saturday morning, we woke up to rain pelting the tent and the Fraser River rushing past our campsite. I could hardly believe my luck.

"It's too rainy to pick today," I told my sleeping parents, whispering as loud as I could over the water noise. They hated it when I made too much noise in the morning, but I didn't see how they could sleep with the racket of the rain anyway. If I were convincing enough, maybe they'd decide to travel east right away. Traveling would be better than sitting around doing nothing, and at least we'd be a few kilometers closer to José.

Papá groaned and sat up in his sleeping bag. "Maybe it'll clear up," he mumbled. "*Ojalá*. I hope so."

It didn't clear though. It got worse and worse, and after a few hours of waiting for dryness—first huddled in the tent, and then sitting in the car—we packed up, looked at the map and planned the route east.

"Maybe we can beat the rain clouds and still do some picking today," Papá said, following the road on the map with his finger.

I hoped there weren't many farms in the next few hundred kilometers. Right now, a single farm looking for fruit pickers would be enough to hold us back for days.

In the backseat, as we drove, I tried to write in my notebook. Even if I'd had a decent story, the road was too curvy for writing, and I couldn't concentrate anyway. All the way across the green, misty Fraser Valley, into the craggy Coastal Mountains, and over the twisty Coquihalla Pass, I prayed for more rain. At least until we got to José's cherry farm.

In the early afternoon, the rain stopped, and so did we. We ate lunch at a picnic table by the highway up in the mountains, halfway between the berries of the Fraser Valley and the fruit trees of the Okanagan. I imagined José's face behind the chain-link fence, and Analía in Mexico City, running toward the mailman, hoping for a letter from me that wouldn't come. I crossed my fingers so tight they hurt.

"At least it's drying out," Papá said when we were on the road again.

Mamá twisted around in the seat to face me. "Sorry we didn't get to your raspberries, *mi amor*. I hope you're not too disappointed." She looked so worried that

71

I almost laughed. Obviously, I was doing a good job of keeping Analía's secret if my own mother couldn't figure out what was going on.

It took a long time for the road to stop climbing and level off. Bit by bit, the mountains looked less craggy. More trees poked up from the hillsides, and after hours and hours of driving, the road sloped down into a valley full of green fields with the sprinklers going. The hills beyond were brown.

I was the first one to see the sign, a fluorescent pink piece of plastic stapled to a telephone pole. Big sloppy black capitals said *CHERRY PICKERS WANTED. CASH.*

"*Llegamos!* We're here!" I shouted, and Papá jumped, jerking the car to the right for a scary moment before he got control again. I didn't know exactly where José's farm was, but if people were advertising for cherry pickers, we had to be close.

"*Tranquila, m'hija!*" His wide eyes met mine in the rearview mirror. "Calm down! Why are you so excited about cherries all of a sudden? I thought strawberries and raspberries were your favorites."

Mamá looked back at me again, suspicious this time. "You've been missing José, haven't you?"

I nodded vigorously. "Maybe we could work at his farm next? I mean, if we're going to pick cherries, we might as well pick them where we already know people, right?"

Mamá gave me a funny look, as though she'd finally realized I was up to something. But by then, it didn't matter what she thought, because we were halfway across the province. Any moment, we'd be at José's farm. "Well, okay," said Mamá. "It does get pretty lonely when everyone is speaking a language you can't understand. And it'll be good to see the others again."

My parents talked about that for a while, and I peered out the window, looking for clues. José's farm could be around any corner. In fact, he could appear on the side of the road at any moment…if he could get out, that is. I pictured the dripping fangs of a huge guard dog at the front gate and shivered.

The road wound up a steep hill, and at the end, a chain-link fence marked the edge of the cherry farm. I scanned the entrance for any sign of José or the other workers but saw only a small dirt parking lot packed full of dusty cars. A little red building stood in one corner with a sign saying *Office*, and behind that stood rows and rows of cherry trees, as far as I could see.

In that second before I stepped out of the car, nothing moved, only a few leaves in the trees. No vicious guard dog. No chained-up farm workers. I felt my face go hot. What if we'd hurried here for nothing?

I stepped out of the car. Nothing happened. I could hear the breeze and feel it against my neck, but that was all.

The longer I'd thought about Analía's letter, the more I'd convinced myself it must be true. But now I was relieved Analía told me not to tell anyone because I'd probably have felt really dumb telling my parents and José what I'd imagined.

"*Hola!*" called a familiar voice. It was Marcos, one of the other men who had worked with my parents in the flower fields. I'd never paid much attention to him and he never seemed interested in anything I had to say. Now I noticed that he looked exhausted. His hair was all straggly, like it needed washing, and he had dark shadows under his eyes. His lips smiled at us, but the wrinkles in his forehead made him look worried.

"Marcos, *cómo estás*?" Papá asked, as if he couldn't see for himself how tired Marcos looked. Adults do that sometimes, ignoring the obvious and asking the question anyway. Papá hugged him, and Mamá kissed Marcos's cheek, as friends do in Mexico.

"*Bien*," Marcos said. "Fine." He reached down a hand and ruffled my hair. I hated it when people did that, and I flinched and almost jumped away when I saw Mamá give me a warning glance.

I ignored her and kept looking around. Where was José (who never ruffled my hair)? He would have asked how my summer was going, what we'd seen so far, and what I thought I'd like about the cherry farm. So far, I definitely thought climbing the trees would be best. From the top, you could probably see clear across the valley. I felt a flutter of excitement. Now *that* would be something interesting to write about. These big bushy trees would be good for hiding in, and I bet I could learn many interesting things from way up in a cherry tree. It would be fun to know what adults talked about when they didn't think I was around.

The adults kept chatting about this and that, until Papá excused himself and stepped into the farm office. A few minutes later, he poked his head out and motioned us in.

"I'll see you later," Marcos said, returning to the cherry trees.

Inside, the office was smaller than it had seemed from the parking lot. The walls were made of fake-looking dark brown wood, like the kitchen cupboards in our basement suite. The desk was covered with stacks of paper, and the man behind the desk—the *patrón*, the farmer—looked small too until he stood up and towered over Papá. The *patrón* had a long white beard and a big belly, like Santa Claus. He said we could head to the far end of the orchard and start picking right away. "Later, you can pitch your tent next to the building where the rest of the Mexicans are staying. Plenty of work here," he added, rubbing the top of his belly. "Some trees on the sunny side are already ripening, and the others only have a few more days to go. You got here just in time."

He was right, in more ways than one.

CHAPTER 10

Cherries

Picking cherries was much more fun than picking strawberries—at least, from down below it *looked* like more fun. Papá wouldn't let me climb the trees because he was afraid I'd fall.

I'd probably climbed more trees lately than the adults had. The park halfway between Julie's house and mine was full of climbing trees, and I was about to say that to Papá when Mamá found me a job, running from ladder to ladder, helping the pickers empty their pails.

I hesitated but decided maybe I'd better start with that. We'd be at this farm for a while anyway, and I'd have plenty of chances to climb trees when my parents weren't looking.

Each picker wore a harness with a bucket on the front so that up in the tree, he could drop in cherry after cherry—*ping, ping, pingpingping*—without losing his balance or spilling the fruit. When the bucket got full, the picker called me, and I raced to that ladder with another bucket and waited for the cherries to be dumped inside. Then I poured them into a big container at the base of each tree.

I liked trying to guess where the next call would come from and who was in each tree, because sometimes the pickers went up so high they disappeared entirely. Meanwhile, I kept an eye out for the flash of José's red and white ballcap through the leaves, and I listened for the sound of his voice.

"He's in another part of the orchard," Mamá said when I got tired of waiting and asked where he was. "The *patrón* wanted him to spray some trees so bugs don't get to the fruit before it's ripe."

"It's only a one-day job though," said Marcos's voice from up inside another tree. "He'll probably be back picking with us tomorrow."

"And you'll see him tonight," said Papá, "when we set up camp. I bet he can hardly wait to ask what his daughter wrote to you in that top-secret note."

He laughed, and I laughed too because, at that moment, it seemed as though Analía had nothing to worry about after all.

"*Allá*," said Marcos. "That's it over there." It was late evening and we'd finished picking. José still hadn't shown up, and Marcos was taking us on a tour of the farm.

I wasn't paying much attention. I was waiting for my lucky break so I could wander toward the trees, as if I saw something interesting on the ground or something unusual in the bark. My parents would be too busy catching up with Marcos and the others to notice. I'd scramble up the tree, take in every detail of the brown valley below, get a deep sniff of the leafy green tree air and hurry down before anyone noticed that I was gone. Then I'd scribble everything into my notebook, and I'd have at least one story.

Papá whistled—a long, slow whistle like he couldn't believe what he was seeing. I looked up, but all I saw was a run-down green building, about half as big as a classroom. A barn for farming equipment, maybe. Nothing to whistle at.

"All of you live there?" Mamá asked. "*Todos*? All eighteen?"

For a moment, I forgot about the trees. They lived *there*? That barn wasn't even big enough to have separate rooms.

"*Sí, señora*," Marcos said. "We all fit in somehow. Bunk beds. Nine of them."

No wonder Marcos looked so tired. Even one loud snorer would make it impossible to sleep.

He led my parents to the building, away from the trees. I tried to stay back, but my mother noticed and took my hand. I shook free, and she stood there, arms crossed over her chest, until I followed. When was this tour going to end?

The bathroom was an outhouse around the back, and the kitchen—if you could call it that—was off to one side. It was only a patch of dirt under a sheet of plastic, with two wooden tables and a few old bookshelves full of dishes. I didn't see a sink or a stove anywhere, but a grimy old fridge stood in one corner. Our campsite by the Fraser River had been nicer. This side of the farm didn't even have much of a view because right behind the outhouse was a barbed wire fence, separating this orchard from the neighbors'.

Trees everywhere and not a moment of privacy to climb them!

"*Sí, señora*," Marcos said, folding his arms across his chest. "This is where we live."

Mamá shook her head.

"You can pitch your tent anywhere you like," said Marcos. "Anywhere except at the back, that is. That's where the showers are. I'd show you now, but someone is probably using them, and one of the doors fell off last week."

Papá frowned. "It can't be fixed?"

"We've tried," Marcos said. "I mean, we tried to ask the *patrón* for something to fix it with, but none of us knew the right English words. He got frustrated and shouted something and stomped off. We kind of gave up after that."

So much for the *patrón* reminding me of Santa Claus, I thought.

"I bet Rosario could help with her English," Papá said.

I pretended to be fascinated by a stone at my feet, but Papá didn't seem to notice. "You should see this kid's marks! She could make her fortune translating for the rest of us."

My face was fiery hot, and I prayed no one would ask me to practice my English.

"I would steer clear of the *patrón*, if I were you," Marcos warned, "no matter how good your English. He flies into a rage at the littlest thing. You should have seen him yelling at Oscar last week. He's got a temper, that man."

No one said anything for a second, and I turned back to look at the trees. That's when I saw José. He wasn't wearing his precious ballcap, and he was walking funny. I called to him and waved, but he didn't wave back; he just sort of staggered in our direction.

I grabbed Mamá's hand, and we ran.

"Sick," he wheezed when we arrived at his side. "Can't breathe." The black parts of his eyes were tiny dots. I looked wide-eyed at Mamá, and she pulled me close, as though it were me, not José, who needed help.

Then Papá and Marcos were there, pulling José's arms around their shoulders to help him walk. They'd hardly taken three steps when José threw up, fell to his knees and threw up again.

Papá beckoned Mamá and me closer. "Guadalupe, you help José," he told her. "Rosario, you come with me. We'll get the car and tell the *patrón* we're going to the hospital."

Cold fear twisted in my stomach. I couldn't argue now, not with José lying on the ground, shaking, while Mamá and Marcos tried to hoist him up. But how could I talk to the *patrón*? A man who yelled at his workers about any little thing would never listen to a kid, especially a kid whose English was sure to come out all wrong. It always did when I was nervous or upset. And yelling the names of vegetables in Spanish wasn't going to help me one bit this time.

José moaned and put his hands to his head, and I knew I didn't have a choice. I put my hand in Papá's, and we flew.

CHAPTER 11

Speak

José didn't want to get into the car.

"The *patrón* will fire me for sure," he said. "And I can't go back to Mexico now, not without my summer's wages. How will my family eat?"

"How will they eat if you return to Mexico dead in a wooden box?" Mamá snapped. "We're not going to sit by and let you die."

My stomach flipped over, and instantly I was back in Mexico, huddled in a corner, trying to understand what had happened to my brother. The people who killed Ricardo hurt him so badly that I wasn't allowed to see the body. Everything changed after that day. Everything.

We had to help José. We couldn't let him die.

José was shaking too much to speak. Marcos and Papá and a few of the other men heaved him into the back of the station wagon. I scrambled in, crouched behind one seat and held José's hand. *We won't let him die, Analía*, I promised. Not that promising would help anything, but it made me feel like there was hope.

And that gave me an idea.

"Analía wrote to me," I whispered to José. "I mean, she wrote to me about this farm. She was worried about you. She heard what you told her mother, and she wanted to make sure you were okay."

He opened his eyes and looked at me with brown eyes whose black dots were now impossibly small. I didn't even know if he could see me out of eyes like that.

"She needs you to be okay," I said, willing myself not to cry. His eyes were closing again. "*Por favor*, José. Be okay."

"Ees José Lopez," Papá said in his terrible English. "Ees berry seek."

I knew Papá was trying his best, but the nurse at the front desk of the emergency ward looked totally confused. We must have looked weird: Mamá and Papá, still in their work clothes, lowering José into a chair, and me standing off to the side, clutching my notebook to my chest, as if it could make me feel strong.

"Ees seek working," Papá said, still trying to explain to the confused nurse. José was shaking again and starting to sway, even though he was sitting down. Mamá bent over him, stroking his cheek and whispering. Papá placed one hand on his shoulder, and the other on my head. "*Cuéntale*, Rosario," Papá said, his face red, and his forehead tight with worry. "*Cuéntale, por favor.*" *Tell her. Please.* But what was I supposed to say? All the way to the hospital, they'd been rapid-firing questions at José. Had he ever been sick like this before? What did he think caused it? What was he wearing when he was spraying the plants? What was he spraying with? Had he been wearing a mask?

None of it made any sense to me, but somehow my parents got it in their heads that José was sick from spraying the cherry trees, even though he'd sprayed plants lots of times before. Back in Victoria, he helped spray the flower fields all the time, and he'd never got sick like this. As far as I could tell, my parents were desperate for an explanation and ready to believe anything.

There didn't seem to be any point telling the nurse about my parents' crazy ideas. If I made it sound like José couldn't handle his work, he might lose his job. Both Analía and José said the *patrón* could kick him out of Canada if he wanted, and then what would José's family do? Starve like other people in Mexico who didn't have jobs?

It was as if my parents hadn't even heard what the *patrón* shouted as we left the farm. After Papá told him we were taking José to the hospital, he wouldn't even open the gate for us, and once Papá had forced it open and we took off, the *patrón* yelled that if we said anything to make him look bad, he'd make sure we never worked in this area again.

"*Por favor*, Rosario," Papá repeated. "*Cuéntale.*"

My heart squeezed painfully tight. I wanted to help, but what could I say that wouldn't make things worse? What if José's sickness had nothing to do with the farm at all, and I said something that got back to the *patrón*? Or what if I opened my mouth to speak and the nurse couldn't understand me, and they gave José the wrong medication, and he died? What if he died all because of me and my not-yet-perfect English?

"I don't know," I whispered in English finally, looking at my shoes. "I don't know."

Immediately, the nurse's eyes were on me. "Can you tell me what happened?" she asked, her voice gentle. She reminded me of Julie's mother. I closed my eyes. Julie's mother would wait patiently and listen. She would do her best to understand. With any luck, this nurse might do the same.

I took a deep breath and spoke in a voice so small that the nurse leaned closer to hear me.

"José works on a cherry farm," I said; then I stopped. Papá squeezed my shoulder. I took another deep breath and continued slowly, so slowly that I imagined the nurse yelling at me to get on with the story. Suddenly, I was aware of how many other people were in the waiting room, people who had no trouble saying what they needed. This nurse could look after any one of them, and if I took too long with my story, she might.

But if I was going to tell it, I'd have to do it carefully, in my own time.

"My parents and I went to dere"—I winced at my mistake—"went to *the* farm today. My parents *th*ink

José is sick because he had to—" Panic rose in my throat. I didn't know the right words, and the nurse was waiting for me, and if I got it wrong…

"He put someting on the trees to make them healty," I said, forcing the words out faster and faster, ignoring all my mistakes. "My parents tink dat is why he is sick now. Dey say he needed someting to cover his mouth and his nose and his hands. On some farms, people wear someting on the face and the hands, but not here. And José did not complain. He did not want to come to the hospital. He needs to work."

The nurse nodded and scribbled notes on paper, not looking up.

I screwed my eyes shut again, thinking frantically. My throat was dry, and my heart was racing. Did I make it clear that it was my parents, not José, who thought he got sick from spraying the plants? Would the nurse write it down that way?

"He must feel better soon," I blurted, no longer caring how my English sounded. "He needs to work so dat his family can eat. In Mexico, he could not find a job. He wants his children to eat and to go to school. Analía wants to be a teacher and her brother wants to work in the city. José came to Canada so his children can do dose tings." And suddenly, I realized something that I hadn't understood before, something that was true for my parents too. "He came so dey do not grow up and work on farms like he does."

I finished speaking and opened my eyes, making a flood of tears stream down my face. I wiped them away fast because I wasn't a kid that cried. Not when we left our town, not when all our stuff got stolen and Papá got hurt, not when we had to live in Guatemala City for almost a year, and certainly not when stupid Robbie Zec made fun of me. I was tougher than that. That's what my brother, Ricardo, had always said: You've got to be tough.

But at the same time, I felt awful. *I'm sorry, Analía. I told all your secrets. I didn't know what else to do.*

"Pesticide poisoning," the doctor said. He was a thin man with square wire glasses, a white coat and an accent that wasn't Canadian. Maybe English was his second language too. He'd become a doctor anyway.

We were all standing around José's hospital bed, a tall one that made me feel tiny. I didn't understand what the doctor was talking about, and I was still clutching my notebook as if it could stop everything from flying apart.

I saw confusion on my parents' faces, and this time I didn't hesitate to ask a question. "I'm sorry," I told the doctor in English. "I do not understand. Could you please explain?"

The words came out fine. I'd talked so much already that night that it was less scary to speak English with strangers. Every time I opened my mouth, my parents looked at me like I was some kind of hero.

"Pesticide poisoning," the doctor said, "means that José was spraying the cherry trees with a special chemical to keep the insects away, but the chemical got into his lungs and onto his skin. Maybe he didn't have a good mask and gloves, or a place to wash after spraying the plants. The farmer should have provided all those things. That's the law, but some people don't pay attention to the law."

I translated all this, and my parents and José asked me questions in Spanish. I turned those questions into English for the doctor. "Will he be able to go back to work soon? How long will he have to stay in the hospital?"

"We want to watch him for a few hours more," said the doctor, "and then you can take him home. He shouldn't go back to work for a week or so though, and he certainly shouldn't do any more spraying."

I froze. The *patrón* wasn't going to let José take a week off work at the height of cherry season. Could I pretend that the doctor hadn't said anything? Maybe the adults wouldn't notice?

The doctor, Papá, Mamá and José all looked back at me, waiting. I shifted from foot to foot and held my notebook tighter, and when I spoke, José scrunched up his eyes like I did sometimes when I was trying not to cry.

"Pack your things," the *patrón* said to José when we arrived back at the farm. He was standing with his arms folded across his chest, like he was holding himself back from exploding. "I can't believe you dared show up here again. My phone has been ringing off the hook. What on earth did you tell them at the hospital? That I'm some mass murderer or something?" He spat on the ground and glared at José. "Farming's tough enough without workers like you. I've booked your ticket back to Mexico. You leave immediately."

I didn't know how much to translate, or how to tell them the bad news. "José," I whispered, while the *patrón* shouted about unreliable workers and people ruining his good name. "He's not making any sense. He says you have to go back to Mexico *right now*. Can't you stay a few days until you're feeling better?"

I expected José to look shocked or angry. Instead he closed his eyes and took a deep breath. He said nothing.

The *patrón* was shouting and waving his arms around, his face red as an overripe strawberry. He no longer looked like Santa Claus. "They don't even listen to me when I'm talking to them!" he bellowed. "Out! Now! You have fifteen minutes to get your things, and then I never want to see you again. Give your name at the bus station, head to Vancouver, get off at the airport and leave this country. You're finished here…you."

I wondered if he even knew José's name.

The farmer stormed off, and the other adults turned to me. I translated quickly without looking anyone in the eye, and when I finished, we were all quiet. My parents looked at each other. Then Mamá hugged me tight, and my father talked to José in whispers. José shook his head. Papá frowned and whispered something else, but José crossed his arms over his chest and shook his head again.

Everything happened quickly after that. We jumped into the car and sped down the gravel road to the little building at the back of the orchard. José gathered his things as fast as he could. The other workers were already picking cherries, and we didn't have time to say good-bye.

The drive to the bus station was a silent one. And that silence felt all wrong. I had too many questions, and we weren't going to see José again for a long, long time. Maybe never. So why did Mamá put a finger to her lips and place a hand on my knee when I tried to talk? Why did no one speak?

CHAPTER 12

The Story

After all the silence in the car, the good-bye at the bus station was a gush of thank-yous and promises. José said he wasn't very good with pen and paper, but Analía would write us letters, and we'd always have a home in Mexico City.

We pretended that my parents and I might one day have enough money to visit Mexico again. We didn't pretend that José would ever return to Canada. The *patrón* had sworn he'd write a letter to the government saying that José was a troublemaker. And who would bring a troublemaker back to Canada?

"I'll be okay," José said at the bus station, crouching down to hug me. "*No te preocupes.* Don't worry. Analía will write to you as often as she can, I'm sure, and you can write to us anytime. I gave your mother the street address and the e-mail."

It wasn't supposed to happen this way. I was supposed to arrive at the cherry farm, see that José was perfectly fine, and let Analía know that she'd been worried for nothing. I wasn't supposed to be saying good-bye to José a few weeks into July with a whole summer of picking left to go.

"Thank you for being such a good friend." He hugged me again. "You and your English saved my life, *sabes*? Keep writing in that notebook of yours. The world needs people like you who can tell our stories."

I nodded but said nothing. All my words, in any language, had left me again.

Papá, Mamá and I waved until the bus disappeared down the road.

"Now what?" I asked when we got back into the car.

"Now we find a campground and sleep for a few hours," Papá said, "and later, we find another farm to work on. A good farm. I'm sure there are many. José had bad luck with that one."

We camped on one of the brown hilltops that I'd wanted to see from the tops of the cherry trees. Most of the people camping there were away harvesting fruit, and the air was quiet, perfect for sleeping.

It was late afternoon before any of us had the energy to get up. Papá said he was going to take a shower while Mamá and I made supper. She didn't speak as she put the food on the table, and when I couldn't stand the quiet anymore, I blurted out one of the questions that had been bothering me all afternoon. "Why did the *patrón* get mad at José for getting sick? The doctor said it wasn't his fault, that he needed a better mask or something."

Mamá finished opening a can of beans. "I know," she said. "And the *patrón* knows that too, but he was afraid people would find out he didn't treat his workers properly. That's why he sent José back to Mexico, even though he wasn't allowed to."

I stared at her. "He wasn't allowed to?"

"No, he wasn't," she said. "When José came to Canada, both he and the *patrón* signed an agreement saying how long José would work here. The *patrón* broke that agreement by sending José away."

"Why didn't you say anything?" I demanded. "Why did you—?"

"José knew," Mamá said. "He knew the *patrón* was breaking the rules by sending him back to Mexico, but what could we do? Who would we complain to? We don't speak English well enough to help him, *mi amor*, and we couldn't make you fight with the *patrón*."

I looked back at her, not knowing what to say.

"You did the most important thing, Rosario," she said, placing a hand on mine. "You saved José's life, and he and his family will be forever grateful to you. You made us very proud."

I shook my head. I wished I'd known who to complain to about the *patrón*, and I wished I'd told the *patrón* what I thought of him. I imagined marching up to his office and telling him how horrible he was. I pictured his furious red face and loud shouts, his fists shaking as he rushed toward me and—

I shivered. Mamá was right. Even with perfect English, I couldn't have fought the *patrón*.

I plunked cutlery onto the table, sat down and propped my head in my hands. I wished we were all back in Victoria, working on the friendly farm, going to the library on Sundays, and living exactly as we had before my impossible traveling idea.

How had I ever imagined that picking our way across the province would give me Normal Canadian Kid stories? Nothing about my life was ever going to be normal. I could see that now.

Papá returned from the shower, walking slowly, as if he didn't have the energy to move faster. He sat down at the table and offered us a weary smile.

"Remember when we went picking with Julie and her mother?" I asked.

"That was a good day," he said.

"I think they had fun," I said. "Julie liked all the colors."

"Remember how Ms. Norton said she never thought about how tulips grow or who picks them?" Mamá smiled at the memory.

Papá took a slice of bread and bit into it. "Why would she?" he asked. "If we could speak English as well as Rosario does, maybe we could tell people our stories, and they would listen, but who has time to learn English when we're this busy working?"

That evening, we drove from one farm to another, comparing them.

I sat in the backseat with my notebook, remembering the first time I met José and everything that had happened since. I wrote down stories he'd told me about his family and about how excited he was to be working in Canada. I wrote about him getting sick and being afraid of being fired, and about Analía. I tried to imagine her all grown up, a teacher with a big smile.

I hoped it was possible. If there was one thing I'd learned, it was that you could never know exactly what was going to happen. I'd tried so hard to keep my English to myself until it was perfect, but it all bubbled out at the hospital. José said I saved his life. No one could have imagined *that* happening.

I wondered what my own life would be like when I grew up. Would I write for a newspaper, or become a doctor like the one who helped José? Maybe I'd be something else that I couldn't even imagine yet. And one day, I might even feel like Canada was home.

I stared out the window at the brown hills with the orange sky behind. If I had had the money, I would have called Julie. I wanted to know what life was like in a skyscraper in Vancouver, and I wanted to tell her about my life here. And after all, if I could speak English to doctors and nurses and an angry *patrón*, I could certainly speak English to my best friend on the phone.

After Peaches

"Look at this!" I shouted.

Julie had barely stepped into our new apartment when I raced across the living room, waving a fat envelope. "Analía's letter arrived this morning," I said. "She put many things in it!"

Sending it from Mexico must have cost her family a fortune, but in her last e-mail, Analía said it was the least they could do to thank us. Besides, José might be working again soon. A tomato packing plant a few hours from his house was looking for workers. He'd have to spend most of his time away, but he could go home every ten days. That was something anyway.

It had been two months now since he went back, and a week since Mamá, Papá and I had finished harvesting peaches and returned to Victoria. Even after a whole summer of picking fruit and saving money, we still couldn't afford a fancy apartment with a swimming pool, but Julie says pools in apartment buildings aren't so great anyway. The one at her father's place turned out to be tiny, and the adults never wanted to share it.

Julie's mum helped us find a bright, sunny apartment with smooth linoleum floors perfect for sliding on, right down the street from her house. As soon as we moved in, I took off to the library to e-mail Analía our new address and to tell her what I needed for my book. Now the envelope had arrived, and Julie looked as excited as I was. We flopped onto the floor, and I pulled out everything I had asked Analía for: hand-drawn maps of her neighborhood, pictures of her house, copies of letters that José had sent from Canada and family photos.

"Wow," Julie said when we'd studied every piece. "Your book will be fabulous. Way more interesting than my story."

"You always say that," I told her, "and then you write something wonderful."

She shrugged. "I know what my cover will look like, at least." From her backpack she pulled four pieces of thick cardboard, a pile of magazines, glue, a roll of clear tape and a brown paper bag. She showed me how she'd crinkled up the bag and rubbed until it was smooth and soft, like an old leather book. "I'm going to glue it to my cardboard and use a fancy pen to write the title, *The Exciting Summer Adventures of Julie Norton.*"

"But I thought you said your summer was boring."

"It was," she admitted, "but you can't let the reader know that. You've got to pretend you have a really good story to tell. No one's going to read a book called *Julie Norton, Lonely in Vancouver.*"

I laughed. "I'm glad we're together again."

"No kidding." She made a fish face at me, and I laughed again.

I went to the kitchen to get scissors and felt markers, and when I came back, Julie was arranging two kinds of cookies on a plate. "Mum made these last night," she said. "A special treat for book-making day."

I looked down at the plate and grinned. Four chocolate-chip cookies sat beside four puffy Mexican *galletitas*.

"She used the recipe your mum gave us," Julie explained, looking a bit worried. "I hope you like them."

I began munching right away. "Delicious," I said, through a mouthful of crumbs. The *galletitas* were heavier than Mamá's, and the flavor was different, but I didn't care. I loved the idea of Ms. Norton making Mexican cookies and not worrying about whether they turned out properly, knowing that we'd appreciate them just because she'd tried.

That's the thing about doing something new: you never know if it's going to work, and it'll definitely take practice. People might even laugh at you, but eventually you'll do it so well that no one will remember your mistakes. Sometimes having the courage to make mistakes is the most difficult thing of all.

Next time Robbie Zec laughs at my mistakes, I'll have a secret weapon: that feeling I had when José said I saved his life. No matter what Robbie thinks, my English was good enough. All the insults in the world can't take that memory away.

I'll write that memory in my book, along with all the others from this summer. Way back in the spring, I wanted my book to look like one you'd buy in a store, but now I prefer one you could never buy anywhere. My cover will be a crazy mixture of magazine clippings, drawings and words—bright and colorful and all my own—and the story inside will be the same. I may not tell it perfectly, but it's mine to tell, and that's what I'm going to do. Just watch me.

Author's Note

In this story, José comes to Canada as part of the Seasonal Agricultural Workers Program (SAWP). Each year, through this program, Canadian farmers bring close to twenty thousand Mexican and Caribbean workers north to Canada to help harvest fruit.

In some ways, the program is good because Canadian farmers get steady workers, and Mexican workers earn enough money to feed their families back home. Sometimes, though, foreign farm workers can find themselves in difficult situations.

The program has specific rules about who is allowed to join. The Mexican worker must have farm work experience and no university education. He or she must have a family waiting back in Mexico. The Canadian government made these rules because it wants the workers to return to Mexico and not to stay in Canada.

The workers who come here have made a hard choice to leave behind their families for much of the year. Once in Canada, they want to work hard to earn as much money as possible. Many workers are afraid of making their bosses angry, because they want to keep their jobs. If a worker is fired, he or she must find a job on another farm or get sent back home. For workers who don't speak English and don't know where to look for help, finding a new job seems impossible, and so they don't complain, even if the boss doesn't treat them well or makes them do dangerous work (like spraying pesticide without a good mask).

Of course, there are always good bosses and bad bosses. In my research for this book, I talked to farmers who gave their workers good homes and healthy workplaces while in Canada. Not every farm worker enjoys that situation though. In this story, I have tried to show both.

The van accident that Rosario's parents talk about in Chapter Eight is based on a crash that really happened in March of 2007, when three farm workers were killed and fourteen were hurt because the van for the farm workers didn't have proper seats or seatbelts.

The details about the cherry farm are based on the combined experiences of many farm workers in British Columbia.

Glossary

Abuela—grandmother

Allá—there

Bien—fine

Cómo estás?—How are you?

Cuéntale—Tell her.

El viejo—the old one

Estofado—stew

Galletitas—cookies

Hicimos suficiente—We made enough.

Hierbas malas—weeds

Hola—hello

Llegamos—We're here.

Loco / loca—crazy

M'hija / m'hijo—my daughter / my son. Some adults use these for any young person, whether their child or someone else's

Mi amor—darling

No te preocupes—Don't worry.

Ojalá—hopefully

Para tí—for you

Patrón—boss, in this case, the farmer

Por favor—please

Qué día—What a day.

Quesadillas—a piece of flatbread (*tortilla*) folded in half with beans or cheese inside.

Sabes—you know

Señor—Mister, sir

Señora—Mrs., madam

Señorita—Miss

Sí—yes

Suficiente—enough

Todos—all, everyone

Tortillas—a flatbread made of wheat or corn

Tranquila—Calm down.

Tu amiga—your friend

Vamonos—Let's go.

Veo veo—the Spanish name for the game "I spy"

Acknowledgments

Many thanks to Erika Del Carmen Fuchs (Justicia for Migrant Workers BC) and Miguel Angel Zenón for their stories, comments and suggestions; to IBBY (International Board on Books for Young People) for the Frances E. Russell Award that helped make this book possible; to Alvera Mulder, Ev Brown, Ruth Copley, Ian Vantreight, Raj Chouhan and Holly Caird for research help; to Susan Braley, Margo McLoughlin, Holly Phillips and Robin Stevenson for their constructive criticism; to Sarah Harvey for her brilliant editing and generosity of spirit; to my husband Gastón Castaño for his love and support; and to our baby girl Maia Elisa Castaño for bringing so much joy to our lives.

When she was growing up, Michelle's favorite spot was the library, so it's no surprise that she studied literature at university. Since graduating, she has cycled across Canada, taught creative writing in the Arctic and married the pen pal she'd been writing to since she was fourteen. She lives in Victoria, British Columbia. For more information about Michelle and her books, please visit her website at www.michellemulder.com.